Sir Orfeo

A Legend from England
retold by Anthea Davies
illustrated by Errol Le Cain

Bradbury Press · Scarsdale, New York

SIR ORFEO

LADY HERODYS

SIR ORFEO

Long ago there lived a king whose name was Sir Orfeo. His people loved him, not only because he was a good king, but because he played the harp so marvellously that men journeyed from far and wide to sit down at the table in his great hall and listen for hours into the night.

When he played, the trees came walking down from the hills, the streams stood still, and the hunted stag and the hounds at its throat all stopped enchanted in their tracks to hear him.

Sir Orfeo had a wife whose name was Herodys and he loved her more dearly than anything in the world.

One day the lady Herodys, with her maidens about her, went out into the orchard, and they sat down beneath an

apple tree. When noon came, Herodys had fallen asleep, and her maidens laid their fingers on their lips and waited, lifting their faces to the sun overhead.

Suddenly Herodys started up with a wild shriek, and ran out of the orchard and into the castle. Her maidens leapt to their feet and streamed after her. They found her in her bedchamber, screaming as if she had gone mad. Someone rushed to fetch Sir Orfeo, and he came to the bedchamber like the wind. At the sight of him Herodys grew quiet, but wept bitterly.

"Dear life, what is the matter?"

"Dear lord, while I slept, a grim king came to me, with a train of knights and ladies, and he asked me to go with him to his kingdom, where there are cities and towers, rivers and forests and fields of flowers. I would not go with him, and I told him as much, but he vowed that tomorrow he would come and fetch me, even if I were guarded by a thousand warriors, and take me away. Love, I must leave you, there's no help for it."

"How can we be parted? We have not been divided from one another since we were betrothed. I will wait for this king with all my army."

The next day at noon Sir Orfeo waited under the apple tree, holding Herodys by the hand; and around them, standing shoulder to shoulder and facing outwards with drawn swords, was Sir Orfeo's army. As the sun stood overhead, Herodys vanished from the midst of them, and no one knew where she went.

Sir Orfeo sought out his oldest counsellor and said, "I will not stay here any longer. I give the kingdom into your charge. When you hear that I am dead, choose another king. Rule well, and do not weep for me."

Then he left the city, barefoot and wearing ragged clothes, and carrying his harp.

He went up on to the bare heath, and lived there, with only the little snakes and birds in the briars for company. He ate herbs and roots, and slept among the rocks in the wind and rain.

Sometimes, when the mist drove over the moors, he thought he heard the sounds of a battle being fought— shouts, and the clamor of weapons, and the dim blowing of a horn. But he never saw anything.

Then one hot day in spring a great hunt went by him, and he ran after it, laughing because he thought he was in a mad dream. No one ever hunted up there on the lonely heath. There were many ladies, all in white, each lady carrying a white hawk on her wrist, and riding a white horse. The last one looked back at him, and it was Herodys. Neither of them spoke, but the tears fell from her eyes to see him, who had been so great a king, look so starved and wild. Then the whole throng swept on and vanished through a huge door that opened in the side of a hill. It closed behind them. Sir Orfeo flung himself against it and beat on it with his fists, crying:

"Let me in! Let me in! I am a minstrel. Let me play my harp before the grim king."

The door opened, and Sir Orfeo found himself in a strange country, flat as a chessboard, with cities and towers, rivers and

forests and fields of flowers. The sky was gold all over and shone dully, and there were no shadows.

He came to the castle of the grim king, and the courtyard was full of people, but they were silent and did not move, for they were in an enchanted sleep.

Sir Orfeo went into the king's hall. The king was seated on a throne, wearing a crown neither of gold nor silver, but wrought out of a single jewel. His court were about him. They had all been stolen away from the world of men, and Herodys was among them.

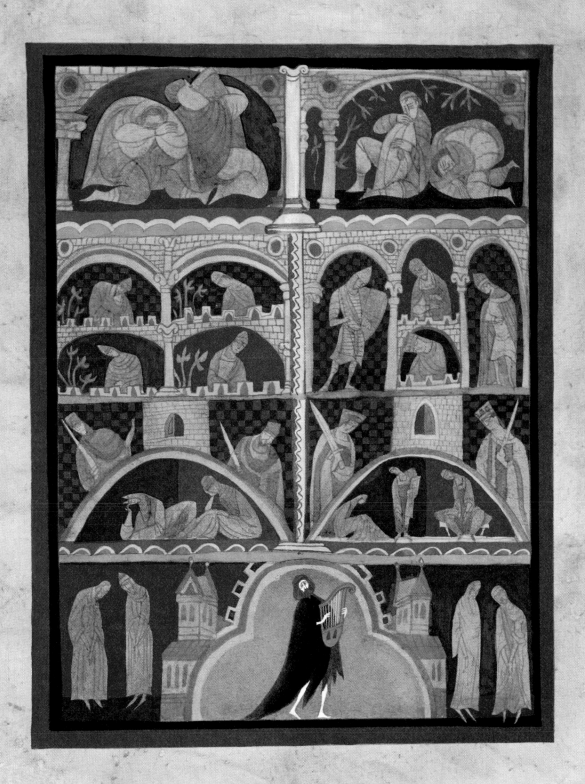

Sir Orfeo stood before the grim king and played his harp. The court fell silent, the sleepers outside came gliding across the courtyard to listen, their still faces staring in at the windows. The king turned his head toward Sir Orfeo as if compelled. He too was spellbound by the music.

"What can I give you?" he said. "How can I reward such a minstrel? Anything you ask I will give you."

"Give me Herodys," said Sir Orfeo.

"She is one of my people now," said the grim king.

"You have promised," said Sir Orfeo. "Is this the worth of the promise of so great a king?"

"I have promised," said the king. "Take her, then, and go."

Sir Orfeo took Herodys by the hand and led her out of the strange country, back to his own little kingdom.

But neither of them knew what had been happening in Sir Orfeo's kingdom while they had been away; whether the oldest

counsellor had despaired of Sir Orfeo's life and chosen a new king, or even seized the throne for himself. Being so unsure of their welcome, they were glad that when they returned no one recognized them.

Sir Orfeo still looked like a beggar, and Herodys drew her hood over her face. They went to the great hall, where the counsellors were feasting, and asked for food. The oldest counsellor had them fed, but when he saw Sir Orfeo's harp, he knew whose it was at once, and said:

"Beggar, where did you find that harp?"

Sir Orfeo answered:

"Where a man lay who had been torn apart by wild beasts."

All the counsellors, griefstricken, hid their faces.

"But he has come to life again," said Sir Orfeo, and he took up the harp and played.

Herodys drew back the hood from her face. One by one
the counsellors raised their heads. At last everyone recognized
them. The table was overturned as they ran out into the streets,

shouting the good news all over the city; and the citizens wept for gladness. Sir Orfeo and Lady Herodys lived happily for many years after, and the kingdom was ruled wisely and well.